THE CHRISTIAN
MOTHER GOOSE
BOOK

UN PETIT ENFANT LES CONDUIRA

C. M. G.

Library of Congress Catalog Card Number: 78-78337
ISBN 0-933724-00-4

First Illustrated Edition, 1978
Second Printing, 1979
Third Printing, Feb. 1980
Fourth Printing, June 1980

THIS BOOK IS GIVEN AS A HAPPY FRIEND

TO *Sarah Skuters*

FROM *Uncle Jim & Aunt Jennie*

THE **CHRISTIAN MOTHER GOOSE** BOOK

Paraphrased Text and Original Text
by
Marjorie Ainsborough Decker

Illustrated by
Glenna Fae Hammond
Marjorie Ainsborough Decker

CHRISTIAN MOTHER GOOSE BOOK COMPANY
P.O. BOX 3838
GRAND JUNCTION, CO. 81501

TO
THE MANY
HANDS AND HEARTS
OF
LOVE AND ENCOURAGEMENT
AND TO
ALL CHILDREN EVERYWHERE
THIS BOOK
IS AFFECTIONATELY
DEDICATED

STORYTELLER'S NOTE

"We spend our years as a tale that is told..." — so says the Scripture.

For hundreds of years, the legendary lady, "Mother Goose" has been telling rhymes and stories to eager children everywhere. Her very name is an instant introduction to a special world that children love.

As a little girl in England, playing and romping to the strains of old rhymes; singing "Rain, rain, go away," as we watched the rain dancing down and really believed our song would send it away; it was far from my thoughts that one day I would gather up those old rhymes for an entirely different purpose.

Last year I returned to England again. As my husband and I stood on the centuries-old bridge across the River Dee, I was warmed to think that the "Jolly Miller" and this ancient bridge had found their way into a book which was the desire of my heart, *The Christian Mother Goose Book.* I could see in my mind's eye the big loaf of bread bobbing down the River Dee—part of a story in the book which links the famous Jolly Miller with the Biblical principle, "Cast your bread upon the waters..." The manuscript had been written and I knew when I returned to America that the lovely thatched roof cottage, a few miles from my childhood home, was the storybook house to grace the front cover.

More of the book came to mind as I visited the Liverpool Museum where a giant mural caught my attention. It was the whimsical "Butterfly's Ball and the Grasshopper's Feast," written in 1807 by the noted Liverpudlian, William Roscoe. However, despite his great achievements in the cultural and economic strength of Liverpool, he is best remembered for this delightful poem written for his little son. What a lesson to learn! That which captivated the children lived on best of all!

Similarly, the charm of "Mother Goose" has captivated children for generations. But this mythical lady seems without anchor in time or homeland.

The origin of most of her simple classics is lost in antiquity. Nevertheless, she has been found on the pages of Shakespeare and Dickens, so we know she must be of very great age.

There is a little book in the British Museum which gives us a hint of her hidden years. This tiny book, measuring only three inches by one and three-quarter inches, crept out of a certain Mary Cooper's publishing house about 1740. It made its way into the streets of London where George II was reigning. He was reputed to be an economical man with a favorite diversion of sitting in his counting house counting out his money. The little book, selling for exactly sixpence, innocently immortalized such royal antics in the nursery rhyme "Sing a Song of Sixpence." It bore the title "Tommy Thumb's Pretty Song Book," and contained thirty-eight rhymes illustrated with woodcuts.

Today, this minute children's book is a cherished treasure; generally acknowledged to be the earliest known book of nursery rhymes.

And so we find the perennial Mother Goose has had multiplied years to teach children many things in her long, storytelling reign of great influence. But the conscience of time and responsibility also rests on her shoulder to bring to children the spiritual side of her personality.

The Christian Mother Goose Book has been sincerely and lovingly written and illustrated so that the endearing "Mother Goose" may also teach little ones the love of God, without which no child is complete.

It is our prayer this book will delight and teach the young—and the young at heart—to know and love Him; and to "live happily ever after..."

Marjorie Ainsborough Decker

MARY'S LAMB

Mary had a little lamb,
  It's fleece was white as snow,
And everywhere that Mary went
  The lamb was sure to go.

Now, Jesus has a little lamb,
  That little lamb is you!
And He is pleased
  When all His lambs
Keep following Him, too.

THERE WAS AN OLD WOMAN

There was an old woman
  Who lived in a shoe.
She had so many children,
  And loved them all, too.
She said, "Thank you, Lord Jesus,
  For sending them bread,"
Then kissed them all gladly
  And sent them to bed.

HUMPTY DUMPTY

Humpty Dumpty sat on a wall,
    Humpty Dumpty had a great fall;
Humpty Dumpty shouted, "Amen!
    God can put me together again."

IF I HAD A DONKEY

If I had a donkey
  That wouldn't go,
Would I beat him?
  Oh, no, no, no!
I'd stroke his little nose
  And give him some hay,
Then tell him I needed him
  To ride a mile away.

8

I SEE THE MOON

I see the moon,
   And the moon sees me.
God bless the moon,
   And God bless me!

THERE WAS A LITTLE GIRL

There was a little girl
   Who found a little pearl,
And then found ten more, twice!
   She sold them all to buy
What her little eye did spy...
   One BIG PEARL of great price!

THREE KIND MICE

Three kind mice,
  See what they've done!
They helped a lost chick
  To find Mother Hen,
They brought some food
  To the church mice, then
They cleaned up the tree house
  For Jenny Wren,
Those three kind mice.

LITTLE LUCY LADYBUG

Little Lucy Ladybug
  How do you take a bath?

Oh, I have a lovely bathtub
  Beside my garden path.
It is a yellow buttercup,
  And when it fills with rain,
I jump into my yellow bath
  And jump out clean again.

Little Lucy Ladybug
  Where do you go to bed?

Oh, I have a lovely bedroom
  Where I lay my little head.
It is a pretty daisy,
  And its sheets are sparkling white.
My pillow is a golden puff
  I sleep on through the night.

Little Lucy Ladybug
  Who cares for you each day?

Oh, I have a lovely Someone,
  And I'll tell you, if I may...
He is the Heavenly Father,
  Who made my bath—and bedroom, too;
And kindly watches over me,
  And cares for me...and you!

TWINKLE, TWINKLE

Twinkle, twinkle, little star,
  God has placed you where you are;
Up above the world so high,
  You're God's light hung in the sky.

Twinkle, twinkle, little star,
  When you look down from afar,
What's the little light you see
  Shining here for God? It's me!

Twinkle, twinkle, little star,
  I can't reach you in a car;
But someday, by Jesus' might,
  I'll fly to visit you each night.

Twinkle, twinkle, little star,
  God has placed you where you are!

JUMPING JOAN

Here am I,
  Little Jumping Joan;
Since Jesus is with me,
  I'm not all alone.

I HAD A LITTLE SYCAMORE TREE

I had a little sycamore tree,
  And what did I see in there?
A little man from Jericho
  Sat perched up in the air!
The King of Heaven's Great Son
  Stopped, and came to visit me;
And all for the sake
  Of the man up in my tree!

LITTLE BOY BLUE

Little Boy Blue,
  Come blow your horn,
The sheep's in the stable
  Where the Savior is born.
Where is the boy
  Who looks after the sheep?
Watching Baby Jesus,
  Fast asleep.

LITTLE BO-PEEP

Little Bo-Peep
 Has lost her sheep
And doesn't know where
 To find them;
But Jesus knows
 And can bring them home,
Wagging their tails behind them.

14

JESUS' FISHY BANK

There was a little fish
   In the Sea of Galilee,
Who played, and ate
   His seaweed greens,
As happy as can be.

Sometimes he peeped at people,
   And kept quiet as a mouse,
As he wondered what they did up there
   Upon the rooftop of his house.

They seemed to ride across it,
    In boats and nets of string;
And when he listened carefully,
    Sometimes he heard them sing...

"Jesus loves the little children,
All the children of the world,
Jesus loves the little children,
All the children of the world."

And that's how he learned of Jesus,
    From the men who sang and fished.
"I wish someday He'd talk to me,"
    His little fish heart just wished.

And then one sunny afternoon,
    When little fishes jump about,
A sparkling, golden coin
    Dropped...Plop!...
Upon his shimmering snout.

A sweet, kind voice said,
    "Little fish,
I've something for you to do.
    Please be a fishy bank for Me,
'Til My friend, Peter, calls on you."

16

The little fish knew right away
   That it was Jesus up there;
So he held on tightly to the coin
   And said, "I'll take good care."
Then Peter came in a day or two,
   For Jesus sent him down,
To reach into the waters blue
   And find that half-a-crown.

The little fish was waiting
   With the coin so faithfully.
And because he was a fishy bank for Jesus,
   He was the happiest fish in all the sea.

17

GOD MADE ME

Did you hear the robins singing,
   "God made me"?
And the crickets chirpy-chinging,
   "God made me."

Did you see the dandelions
   Blowing off their heads with glee?
And flying in the air shouting,
   "God made me!"

Don't you see the trees all swaying,
   Keeping time so prettily;
While bumblebees and beetles
   Sing together, "God made me."

Oh, look at the glowworms glowing,
   Flashing sparks from tree to tree;
Staying up with lighted signs
   Twinkling, "God made me."

Oh, all the little creatures
   Flying, buzzing merrily;
Singing loud from morn 'til night,
   "God made me!"

18

HOW DO EASTER LILIES HEAR?

My mommy had an Easter plant,
  But the flowers were closed up tight.
I wondered when they would open,
  So I watched it day and night.

I watched it on Good Friday
  And all day Saturday, too.
But the flowers stayed all locked up,
  So I fell asleep—wouldn't you?

But then on Easter morning,
  Right before my sleepy eyes,
There were six white Easter lilies;
  What a beautiful surprise!

Who told them it was Easter
  In the darkness of that room?
I didn't know that lilies could hear
  When God told them to open and bloom.

BLESS MY LITTLE FRIENDS

Bless my little friends, dear Jesus,
   Bless the people everywhere.
Bless my puppy, bless my cat,
   And bless my little rocking chair.

HICKORY, DICKORY, DOCK

Hickory, dickory, dock,
   The church mouse ran up the clock.
The clock struck ten,
   The mouse said, "Amen,"
   Hickory, dickory, dock.

SEE, SAW, SACARADOWN

See, saw, sacaradown,
  Which is the way to Zion town?
Up the narrow way, not down,
  That is the way to Zion town.

LITTLE JACK HORNER

Little Jack Horner
  Sat in a corner,
Reading his Bible each day;
  He learned what it said,
And each night in bed,
  The verses he learned he would say.

The first night he said:
  "Since God so loved us
We should love one another."
The next night he said:
  "Obey Father and Mother."
At the end of the week
  He had learned verse seven,
That Jesus is the way to Heaven.

21

TOM, TOM, THE PIPER'S SON

Tom, Tom, the Piper's son,
   Stole a pig and away did run;
The Lord said,
   "Tom, take it back right away,
Or you'll never be happy,
   Day after day."

THERE WAS A CROOKED MAN

There was a crooked man
   Who walked a crooked mile.
He never could straighten up,
   So never did smile.
He found a little book
   That said, "God makes
The crooked straight!"
   He believed,
And straightened up with smiles
   And jumped the garden gate!

TWEEDLEDUM AND TWEEDLEDEE

Tweedledum and Tweedledee
  Once had a quarrel;
For Tweedledum said Tweedledee
  Had pushed him off a barrel.
Said Tweedledee to Tweedledum,
  "I'm very, very sorry."
Said Tweedledum to Tweedledee,
  "I'll forgive you in a hurry."

PETER, PETER

Peter, Peter, Simon Peter,
  Walked on water, totter-teeter.
At first he walked and teetered well,
  Then got afraid and—totter!—fell!
But Jesus reached out with His hand
  And brought him safely back to land.

GRANDMA AND ME

Grandma told me
  She used to be
A little girl
  Who looked like me.

She had a big,
  Brown teddy bear,
And a cuddly doll
  With golden hair.

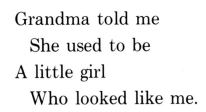

She told me
  That she used to pray,
And thank God
  For her food each day.

And one day
  When she was just seven,
Her daddy told her
  The way to Heaven.

And on that birthday
  Long ago,
She told the Lord
  She loved Him so.

And now that I
  Am nearly seven,
She told me, too,
  God's way to Heaven.

Oh, I believe
  What Grandma said.
Her Bible she has
  Read and read.

And she is good
  And kind to me,
As God wants all
  Grandmas to be.

SING, SING

Sing, sing…
   What shall I sing?
The world is so full
   Of wonderful things!

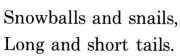

Snowballs and snails,
Long and short tails.

Chirpy chipmunks,
And elephant trunks!

Puddles and streams,
Dancing sunbeams.

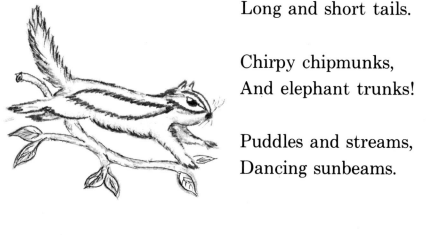

26

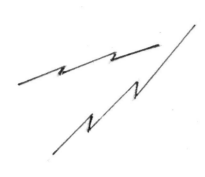

A camel's hump,
Grasshoppers that jump!

Pumpkins so big,
Sandcastles to dig.

Crabs folding under,
Lightning and thunder.

Clouds looking funny,
Bees making honey.

Sing, sing...
   I know what I'll sing!—

"God can make hundreds
   Of anything!"

THIS IS THE ARK
THAT NOAH BUILT

This is the Ark that Noah built.

This is the salt
That lay in the Ark
    That Noah built.

This is the goat,
That ate the salt
That lay in the Ark
    That Noah built.

This is the stoat,
That followed the goat,
That ate the salt
That lay in the Ark
    That Noah built.

28

This is the lamb,
That followed the stoat,
That followed the goat,
That ate the salt
That lay in the Ark
  That Noah built.

This is the ram,
That followed the lamb,
That followed the stoat,
That followed the goat,
That ate the salt
That lay in the Ark
  That Noah built.

This is the goose,
That followed the ram,
That followed the lamb,
That followed the stoat,
That followed the goat,
That ate the salt
That lay in the Ark
  That Noah built.

29

This is the moose,
That followed the goose,
That followed the ram,
That followed the lamb,
That followed the stoat,
That followed the goat,
That ate the salt
That lay in the Ark
  That Noah built.

This is the puppy,
All white and fluffy,
That followed the moose,
That followed the goose,
That followed the ram,
That followed the lamb,
That followed the stoat,
That followed the goat,
That ate the salt
That lay in the Ark
  That Noah built.

This is the cow,
That gave some milk
To feed the puppy,
All white and fluffy,
That followed the moose,
That followed the goose,
That followed the ram,
That followed the lamb,
That followed the stoat,
That followed the goat,
That ate the salt
That lay in the Ark
  That Noah built.

This is Noah's wife,
All dressed in silk,
Who milked the cow,
That gave some milk,
To feed the puppy,
All white and fluffy,
That followed the moose,
That followed the goose,
That followed the ram,
That followed the lamb,
That followed the stoat,
That followed the goat,
That ate the salt
That lay in the Ark
That Noah built.

This is Noah,
As we've said before,
Who built the Ark
That saved his wife,
All dressed in silk,
Who milked the cow
That gave some milk,
To feed the puppy,
All white and fluffy,
That followed the moose,
That followed the goose,
That followed the ram,
That followed the lamb,
That followed the stoat,
That followed the goat,
That ate the salt
That lay in the Ark
That Noah built.

This is the rain
That brought the flood
That covered the earth,
As God said it would;
And so called Noah,
As we've said before,
Who built the Ark
That saved his wife,
All dressed in silk,
Who milked the cow
That gave some milk,
To feed the puppy,
All white and fluffy,
That followed the moose,
That followed the goose,
That followed the ram,
That followed the lamb,
That followed the stoat,
That followed the goat,
That ate the salt
That lay in the Ark
  That Noah built.

This is the rainbow
In the sky,
That followed the Ark
When the earth was dry.
God gave the rainbow
That we should
Remember—
There'll never be a flood,
Like the one
When everything, two-by-two,
Went into the Ark
    That Noah built!

33

IPSEY WIPSEY SPIDER

Ipsey Wipsey Spider,
 Climbing up the spout.
Little Miss Muffet said,
 "Keep on—don't doubt!"
Ipsey Wipsey Spider
 One foot at a time,
Reached the tip-top
 In the bright sunshine!

JACK BE NIMBLE

Jack be nimble,
 Jack be quick,
To bring your Mommy
 A flower you've picked.

34

LITTLE TOMMY TITTLEMOUSE

Little Tommy Tittlemouse
  Lived in a little house,
Built on a Rock
  That would stand, stand, stand.

Little Danny Dormouse
  Lived in a storehouse,
Built on a mound
  Of sand, sand, sand.

Then the rains came like a flood!
Which house do you think stood?

Crash! Bash! Danny's fell!
  Tommy's stayed up very well!

DANDELION SEA

Once upon a time
  There was a happy little place
Called Dandelion Sea,
  Where tiny bugs
And leaping frogs
  Lived together, joyfully.

They had shops and streets,
  And birthday treats,
Like little girls and boys;
  And Grandpa Mole
At the edge of the pond
  Made them whistles, flutes and toys.

Charlie Cricket was the mailman,
  Who jumped from house to house,
Chirping, "Good day!"
  To all his friends,
And taking cheese to Mrs. Mouse.

Barney Beetle was the baker,
  Baking nutty, whole-wheat bread.
"Indeed, it was the most scrumptious loaf
  I've ever eaten," Robin Redbreast said.

When the sun went down
  Each night about eight,
Then the band in the town would meet;
  And the little lightning bugs would bring
Their lights to lighten each street.

The ladybugs played violins,
  And the beetles banged their drums,
The frogs and toads played bass guitars,
  And the hummingbirds all hummed.

But best of all
   Was the end of the week,
When Sammy Sparrow would ring
   The church bell.
And then the whole town
   Of Dandelion Sea
Would listen to Rabbit tell
   How God made all the creatures great,
And creatures very small,
   And made a home for all of them
Because He loves them all.

JACK AND JILL

Jack and Jill
    Went up the hill
To fetch a pail of water.
    A man there said,
"If you drink this,
    You'll still be thirsty after."

"But there is water Jesus gives,
    So won't you ask Him first,
To give you LIVING WATER
So that you will never thirst."

Up Jack got
    And home did trot,
A whole mile and a quarter,
    To tell the GOOD NEWS
To his friends,
    About God's LIVING WATER.

40

LAVENDER'S BLUE, DILLY, DILLY

Lavender's blue, dilly, dilly,
　　Lavender's green,
Teach me to say, dilly, dilly,
　　John 3:16.
God loved the world, dilly, dilly,
　　He gave His son,
To give His life, dilly, dilly,
　　For everyone.

Lavender's blue, dilly, dilly,
　　Lavender's green,
Here comes the King, dilly, dilly,
　　In clouds He's seen.
I'll wear my best, dilly, dilly,
　　My whitest gown,
The King will give, dilly, dilly,
　　To me a crown.

41

GRANDPA'S BIBLE

My Grandpa has a Bible
  That he keeps upon his table;
And when I grow big
  I'll open it
And read it…when I'm able.

When Mommy takes me visiting
  I climb on Grandpa's knee,
And he opens up the Bible
  So the pictures I can see.

There's a picture of Baby Moses
  In a basket, fast asleep.
And one of David carrying back home
  A little sheep.

There's a picture of a wooden ship
  With animals going in;
I like the tall giraffes and goats
  With whiskers on their chin.

HE WHO CUTS
HIS OWN WOOD
IS WARMED TWICE

There's a horse and chariot in the sky—
  That must be fun to ride!
And a picture of a big, big fish
  Which has a man inside.

I saw a man in long, blue clothes
  Writing with a feather!
And lions with some baby lambs,
  All sleeping close together.

Most of all I like to see
  The boy who gave his bread
To Jesus, so that all the hungry
  People could be fed.

Oh, I love my Grandpa's Bible,
  And I love the pictures, too!
Dear Grandpa told me God had sent it,
  So it's very, very true.

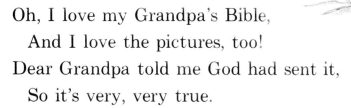

Jesus came from Heaven
To love and help me,
  Yes, I know.
I know because
My Grandpa's Bible
  Told me so!

MISTRESS MARY

Mistress Mary, quite contrary,
How does your garden grow?
God sends rain and sun,
And then one by one
The flowers pop up in a row.

I CAN'T SEE THE WIND

I can't see the wind,
　　But I see what it blows:
Balloons in the air
　　And Mommy's washed clothes.
I can't see God's Spirit
　　Blowing down from above,
But I see how He blows
　　Our home full of His love.

THE OLD WOMAN
IN A BASKET

There was an old woman
  Tossed up in a basket,
Nineteen times as high as the moon.
  And where she was going
I couldn't but ask it,
  For she was saying,
"I must find the way soon!"

"Old woman, old woman,
  Old woman," said I,
"Where are you flying
  Up so high?"
"To find heaven's door,"
  She said with a sigh.

"Oh, come back down,
  I'll show you," said I.
"Here is the Door,
  It's not in the sky.
The Door is dear Jesus,
  And He hears your cry,
HE'LL take you to heaven,
  By and By."

LUCY LOCKET

Lucy Locket lost her pocket,
Kitty Fisher found it;
She was honest,
So she took it back
With ribbon round it.

LITTLE TOMMY TUCKER

Little Tommy Tucker
  Sang for his supper.
What was the song
  That he sang
For bread and butter?

"God is so good,
  And God cares for little Tom."

That's what he sang
  Down to the last crumb.

BENJAMIN BUMBLEBEE'S
ADVENTURE

A little drop of rain
   Fell in Dandelion Sea,
Right on the head
   Of Benjamin Bumblebee.

Now, Benjamin was gathering
   Some honey from a flower,
And said to himself,
   "Oh, it's just a little shower."

And then the sound of church bells
   Came ringing loud and clear,
And he knew that Sammy Sparrow
   Rang the bells for bees to hear.

He knew the bells were saying,
   "Fly quickly to Rabbit's umbrella;
Get underneath it or the rain
   Will wash you to Gopher's cellar!"

"I can take care of myself...I think...
  I don't need to hurry back ,"
Benjamin said, as he buzzed along;
  But the sky was turning black.

Then THREE BIG drops of rain
  Fell on Benjamin's small head;
And all at once, he was soaking wet.
  "I'd better get home!" he said.

But the big, black cloud then burst in two,
  And the rain made one big river.
And there was Benjamin floating away,
  All wet, all cold, all a-shiver.

"I wish I'd obeyed when I heard the bells,
  And flew to Rabbit's umbrella.
Everyone there is safe and dry,
  And I'm washing into a cellar!"

G. GOPHER
KEEP OUT!!

Now, back in town, in Dandelion Sea,
  Under Rabbit's red umbrella,
The other bees ate honey cones,
  Strawberry and vanilla.

"Where is Benjamin?" Rabbit said;
  "He must have stayed out in the rain.
He should be with us under cover,
  But he has disobeyed again!"

"I saw him in the clover field
  By Grouchy Gopher's place,"
Henry Honeybee spoke up,
  With honey cone on his face.

"Oh, dear! then he was washed away!—
  I must get Grandpa Mole
To rescue him before he drowns
  In Grouchy Gopher's hole."

50

So Rabbit ran to Grandpa Mole's
  To tell of Benjamin's plight.
"I'll go save him," Grandpa said,
  "But I need a bright flashlight."

"Take two lightning bugs with you
  And put one on each ear,"
Rabbit said."They will help you
  See the way more clear."

So Grandpa Mole, who swims so well,
  Went quietly down the stream,
With two bright lightning bugs
  Like headlights, lit up all agleam.

They went down under water,
  And followed Gopher's trench,
'Til they came into his cellar
  Where Benjamin was, all drenched!

He was bobbing in the water
  That had washed him underground,
Crying in his bumblebee tears,
  "I know I'll never be found!"

Just then, he saw the lights of
  Luke and Larry Lightning Bug,
And on Grandpa Mole's brown, tiny ears
  They gave a little tug.

"There he is!" they shouted,
  And lit up as bright as could be,
So that Grandpa Mole could see at once
  It was Benjamin Bumblebee.

Poor little Benjamin couldn't fly,
  He'd thought it was the end.
But here in Grouchy Gopher's cellar
  Had appeared his dearest friend.

Grandpa Mole then picked him up,
  Dripping wet and cold,
And placed him on his own warm nose
  And said, "You're safe inside my fold."

He swam so quietly out again,
  Luke and Larry on each ear,
And his nose out of the water,
  With Benjamin riding there.

At last they crossed the clover field
  And climbed back up the hill,
Where they could see that everyone
  Sat under cover still.

Right then, the sun came out so warm
  And dried off Benjamin's clothes.
"If you're feeling better," Grandpa said,
  "You can get down off my nose."

"Thank you, friend, for saving me
  From drowning in the cold.
I promise you, dear Grandpa Mole,
  That I'll now do as I'm told!"

Three days later...

A little drop of rain
     fell in Dandelion Sea,
Right on the head
     of Benjamin Bumblebee.
          BUZZZZ...
He flew back right away
     To Rabbit's red umbrella,
And while it rained
     Ate honey cones,
That happy little fella!

I'M A HAPPY RINGING BELL

Put your fingertips together,
  Now, raise them high up
In the air,
  'Til they look just like
A Steeple,
  And your head's a bell in there.

Turn your head
  From side to side,
It's a bell that says,
  "Ding-Dong."
Ring your bell
With all your might,
And make it sing
  This happy song:

"I'm a happy ringing bell,
I'm a happy singing bell,
Singing, jingling,
Ringing for the Lord."

"Ding, dong, ding, dong,
Ding, dong, ding, dong."

55

PAT-A-CAKE

Pat-a-cake, pat-a-cake,
　Baker's man,
Bake me a cake
　As fast as you can.
Pat it and prick it,
　And mark it with G,
Put it in the oven
　For God and me.

BAA, BAA, BLACK SHEEP

Baa, baa, black sheep.
　Have you any wool?
Yes, sir, yes, sir,
　Three bags full:
One for my master,
　One for the Lord, too,
And one for the little boy
　Who says, "Thank you!"

GOOSEY, GOOSEY, GANDER

Goosey, goosey, gander,
  Where do you wander?
Upstairs and downstairs
  To watch, and to ponder
All the little children
  Saying Good Night Prayers,
And see their mommies kiss them,
  Then tip-toe down the stairs.

FEE, FI, FO, FUM

Fee, fi, fo, fum,
  I smell cookies
That smell yum-yum.
  Be they oatmeal
Or gingerbread,
  Before I eat them
I'll bow my head.

IF

If all the world were paper
  And seas were ink so blue,
We couldn't write enough to tell
  How much that God loves you.

THE LITTLE PUPPY AND JESUS

I'm just a little puppy
  Who gets under people's feet.
And one day a man called Jesus
  Came walking down our dusty street.

I nipped and bit His sandals,
  But He didn't shout at me.
He smiled and picked me up
  And stroked my back, so lovingly.

I felt so safe and happy
  Cuddled up inside His arm;
I knew it was the safest place
  In all the world, from harm.

And then He called me Fido;
  But how did He know my name?
There was no one there to tell Him,
  But He knew me, just the same.

We walked along together,
  And I licked Him on the chin.
He squeezed me closer to Him,
  And I think I saw Him grin!

At last we came to the seashore,
  By the Sea of Galilee,
And I fell asleep in the sunshine,
  Snuggled right upon His knee.

When I woke up and looked around,
    There were lots of girls and boys;
Jumping around and clapping hands,
    And making so much noise.

A man came along to chase them away,
    But Jesus said, "Let them be;
For I am the Friend of these children,
    So let them all come unto Me."

We had such a fine day together
    Jesus, the children and me;
And we played and sang and had some lunch,
    And splashed in the warm, blue sea.

Then came time for boys and girls
    To all go home, you see;
But I didn't have a home at all;
    So what would become of me?

I looked up at dear Jesus,
    To see what my Friend would do;
Then He picked me up and gave me to
    A fine little boy—just like you!

He said, "Take good care of Fido
    And treat him as your friend.
Give him food and water,
    And I will bless you, in the end."

I love that Man called Jesus,
    And I hope you love Him, too.
Because He loves little puppies like me,
    And, of course, boys and girls like you!

YOU ARE SPECIAL

You are very, very special;
　　There is no one just like you!
God made you just the way you are,
　　When He specially thought of you.
He wanted so many children,
　　And not one to be the same,
So that you could be a special you,
　　With a very special name.
So He put a special mark upon your feet
　　And fingers, too!
And of all the children everywhere
　　No one has that mark, but you!
So, smile your very special smile,
　　And give Dad your special squeeze.
Help Mommy with your special hands,
　　(And it's special to say,
　　"Thank you," and "Please.").
Then to every SPECIAL little girl,
　　And every SPECIAL little boy,
God has given a SPECIAL HEART
　　To put His love in to enjoy.

THE BELLS OF LONDON

Oranges and lemons,
Say the Bells of St. Clements;

God made big red apples,
    Say the Bells of Whitechapel;

He made rain and snow
    Says the big Bell of Bow;

The world's in His hands
    Say the Bells of St. Anne's;

He never will fail me
    Say the bells of Old Bailey;

Crown Him with Crowns,
    Say the bells over town.

Ding, dong, ding, dong;
Ding, dong, ding, dong.
Crown Him with Crowns
Say the bells over town.

THE SMILEY SAROO

High up in a swing
   In Tinkertoy Town,
A boy named Bobby
   Just started to frown.

But a funny bird,
   Called a Smiley Saroo,
Pulled up Bobby's lips
   And Bobby smiled, too!

Now, a Smiley Saroo
   Has a smile you can catch,
And wherever he goes
   Children smile, by the batch!

It is said that the smiles
   He started in town,
Have chased away hundreds
   And hundreds of frowns.

He began with a boy
   Who caught the first smile;
Then a girl caught one, too!
   And passed on a big pile.

And before you knew it,
   Why! Folks everywhere,
Had all caught the smiles
   And were smiling out there.

From our house to your house
   And over the hill,
There are long lines of smiles
   That keep catching on, still!

And that Smiley Saroo
   Who started the smiles,
Has now covered the world
   With his smiles-by-the-miles.

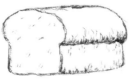
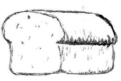

THE JOLLY MILLER

There was a Jolly Miller
  Who lived by the River Dee;
He worked and sang while baking bread,
  A happy man was he.

One day he baked a loaf so big,
  The best he'd ever seen;
"I should never sell this loaf," said he,
  "But wrap it and keep it clean."

He put it on his wooden cart,
  And wheeled it right along;
And as he pushed it to his home
  He sang his miller song:

  "Oh, I'm a Jolly Miller,
  And I bake some jolly bread,
  So that all the jolly people
  Can be jolly-well, well-fed."

FRESH BREAD

Just then, he passed a lassie,
   Who was Mrs. Sarah's daughter;
She was singing, oh, so sweetly,
   "Cast your bread upon the water."

"Cast your bread upon the water,
Cast your bread upon the water,
Cast your bread upon the water,
It will come back twice as big!"

The Jolly Miller stopped his cart,
   And wondered at what she said!
"Did she mean that I should cast away
   My biggest and best loaf of bread?"

"Young lady, now, I ask you,
   Why do you sing such a song?
To throw my bread into the river
   Might be very, very wrong."

Now, Mrs. Sarah's daughter,
   Who could sing just like a bird,
Replied, "My dear Jolly Miller,
   I am singing from God's Word."

"It is written in the Bible
   If we give our bread away,
God will bless it and then bring
   It back again, someday."

"If God has written it,
    Then it's true," the Jolly Miller sighed.
So he turned his wooden cart around
    And went to the riverside.

With a little tear in his jolly eye,
    He tipped his cart by a tree;
And that big loaf of bread
    Went bob-bob-bobbing down the River Dee.

It bobbed along all day and night
    'Til it came to Dandelion Sea,
Where Charlie Cricket, the town's mailman,
    Saw it first and said, "Gracious me!"

He ran with his mail to Mrs. Mouse,
    Then to Grandfather Mole he sped;
"Come quickly and see what has floated in!
    It's a mountain of golden bread!"

Before you could say, "Fee-Fi-Fo-Fum,"
   The news went through all the town.
And as the sun came up, from each house and street
   Came little creatures in nightcaps and gowns.

Then Brother Rabbit came hopping by
   And said, "Well, bless the Lord!
This is enough bread for all of us,
   And much more than we could afford!"

"Bring your baskets and fill to the top.
   No one need go hungry," he said;
"And God bless the man, wherever he is,
   Who sent this wonderful bread."

So all the town of Dandelion Sea
   Went home to breakfast, to dine
On golden pieces of crusty bread,
   That gleamed like bright sunshine.

When Sidney Squirrel and his friends
    Had filled each hollow tree,
The loaf of bread grew big again,
    And went bobbing out to sea.

It sailed along to Blossom Bay,
    Then down to Chipmunk Chigger,
And everytime it fed a town,
    It sailed away much bigger!

At last it came back to the town
    Beside the River Dee.
The Jolly Miller at his work
    Said, "What is this I see?"

"My loaf of bread is twice as big!"
    Then he ran out of the door,
And laughed and clapped his jolly hands,
    And sang his song as before:

"Oh, I'm a Jolly Miller,
    And with this big loaf of bread,
All the jolly, jolly people
    Can be jolly-well, well-fed!"

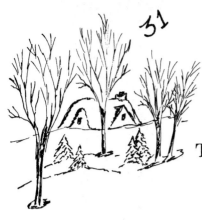

THE MONTHS RHYME

Thirty days hath September,
  Thirty days to remember,
    God loves you!

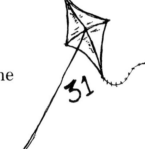

Thirty days, too, has April and June
  Thirty each to sing this tune,
    "God loves me!"

Thirty days hath November,
  Thirty days to remember
    God loves you!

January, March, July and May
  Have thirty-one days for you to say,
    "We love Him!"

August, October and December
  Have thirty-one days to remember,
    God loves you!

February only has twenty-eight,
  Twenty-eight days for you to state,
    "We love Him!"

But in Leap Year there's some extra time,
  When February then has twenty-nine,
  Twenty-nine days to remember,
    God loves you!

WHY DON'T BIRDS WEAR
COATS IN WINTER?

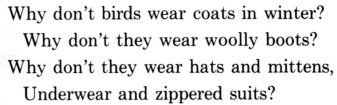

Why don't birds wear coats in winter?
  Why don't they wear woolly boots?
Why don't they wear hats and mittens,
  Underwear and zippered suits?

All they have is colored feathers,
  Winter, spring and summer, too.
Why don't birds wear coats in winter?
  Oh, I wish, I wish I knew!

Boys like me, we have to dress up
  Warm and cozy from the snow.
How Cock Robin flies about without a coat,
  I do not know.

I will tell you
How the birds can live
Without those clothes.
God warms them
From their tiny feet
Up to their tiny nose.
Some He sends away
For winter,
To the lands
Of sunshine bright;
And those He keeps
At home with you,
He keeps warm
Day and night.

Why don't birds wear coats in winter?
  That little sparrow at my door?
God, who made them, keeps them cozy.
  So I'll not worry anymore.

SIMPLE SIMON

Simple Simon met a Pieman
　Going to the fair.
Said Simple Simon to the Pieman,
　"Can you count your hair?"

Said the Pieman to Simple Simon,
　"No one can count hairs, son."
Said Simple Simon to the Pieman,
　"God counts them, every one!"

Simple Simon went to school
  To ask the master there,
"Can you count all of the stars
  And tell me the number, sir?"

Said the master to Simple Simon,
  "There is no way to count."
Said Simple Simon to the master,
  "God knows the whole amount!"

Simple Simon met a climber
  Climbing peaks, one day.
Said Simple Simon to the climber,
  "What does this mountain weigh?"

Said the climber to Simple Simon,
  "No one knows that, I'm afraid."
Said Simple Simon to the climber,
  "God weighed it when it was made!"

SEE-SAW, MARGERY DAW

See-saw, Margery Daw,
   Jackie has found a new Master.
His Name is Jesus, Shepherd and Friend,
   And Jackie's a sheep in His pasture.

LITTLE MISS MUFFET

Little Miss Muffet
  Sat on a tuffet,
Thanking Jesus for curds and whey;
  There came a big spider
And sat down beside her,
  To listen to Miss Muffet pray.

She said…

"Thank you, Lord Jesus,
For good things to eat.
  For berries and nuts
And apples, so sweet.
  I really can't see
How you feed this big world;
  The lions and tigers
And pigs with tails curled.
  The puppies and rabbits,
The birds in the air,
  The horses and cows,
You give them a fair share.
  The sheep and the cats
On your food they dine;
  So thank you, Lord Jesus,
For my kitty's food and mine."

Little Miss Muffet
  Sat on a tuffet,
Thanking Jesus
  For curds and whey;
And then that big spider
  Who listened beside her,
Knelt down with Miss Muffet to pray.

78

ONE MISTY, MOISTY MORNING

One misty, moisty morning,
  When cloudy was the weather,
There I met an old man
  Clothed all in leather.
I put my hand beneath his arm
  And helped him through the rain.
He said, "I thank you, thank you, child,
  And thank you, once again."

BOBBY SHAFTOE

Bobby Shaftoe's gone to sea,
  To pray upon his little knee
That boys and girls will come to see
  That Jesus really loves them.

Bobby Shaftoe's kind and good,
  He helps his daddy bring in wood;
He obeys Mother, as he should,
  Happy Bobby Shaftoe.

HOW PRAISE SAVED
BENJAMIN BUMBLEBEE

One sunny summer morning,
  In Dandelion Sea,
As Charlie Cricket delivered mail
  He heard a voice say, cheerily…

"Hello, there, Mr. Mailman,
  Is this Dandelion Sea?
I just flew in to get some help
  For Benjamin Bumblebee."

"He's lost inside a pipe organ
  And can't find his way out;
The noise he's making down in there
  Is booming out each spout!"

80

"The pipe organ is in a church
  In Dippley Dockerlee,
And when Benjamin came visiting
  He flew down Pipe Number Fifty-Three!"

"He kept five towns awake last night
  With his buzzing in those pipes.
And I heard him say, 'Please get some help,
  I've nearly buzzed off all my stripes.'"

"Poor Benjamin! He needs us,"
  Charlie said. "I'll take a stand.
But may I ask your name, sir,
  And if you'll shake my hand?"

"Oh, please forgive me, Charlie!
  Of course, you wonder who I must be.
Well...my name is Dippley Dock
  And I'm from Dippley Dockerlee."

"In Dippley Dockerlee
  We have flocks and flocks and flocks,
Of roly-poly Docker bugs
  Which sound like little clocks."

"But now we can't hear ourselves tick
    In Dippley Dockerlee,
Because of all that booming noise
    From Benjamin Bumblebee!"

Charlie said, "What can we do?
    What can be quickly sent,
So that Benjamin can find his way
    Out of that instrument?"

"Well, Charlie, we've done all we can
    To find him in two days,
But still we haven't got him out;
    I think we should try Praise!"

"The Bible says we should praise God,
    For praising brings His power.
In everything we should give thanks;
    Let's start this very hour!"

So Charlie Cricket and Dippley Dock
    Told Brother Rabbit right away,
"Tell everyone and everything
    To praise for Benjamin today."

82

Then soon within that very hour
The news went everywhere;
And clouds of sounds of praising God
Went floating in the air...WITH...

Bees a-buzzing,
Butterflies flitting,
Grasshoppers hopping,
Frogs a-jumping,
Roosters crowing,
Spiders swinging,
Birds a-singing
"PRAISE THE LORD!"

Dogs a-barking,
Sheep a-bleating,
Donkeys braying,
Cows a-mooing,
Squirrels chattering,
Hens a-cackling,
Ducks a-quacking
   "PRAISE THE LORD!"

Geese a-honking,
Turkeys gobbling,
Cats meowing,
Pigs a-grunting,
Crickets chirruping,
Chipmunks cheeping,
Mice a-squeaking
    "PRAISE THE LORD!"

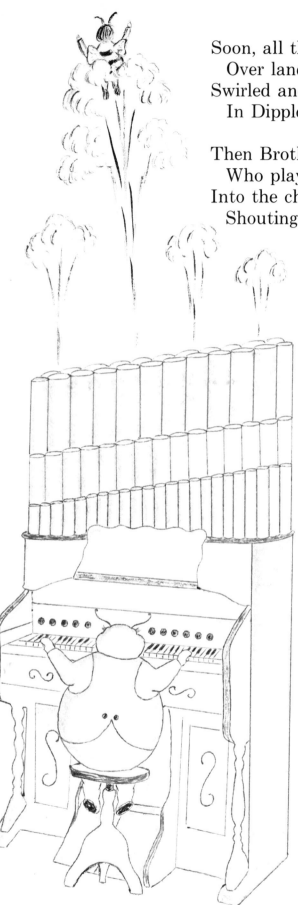

Soon, all the sounds of praise and praise
  Over land and over sea,
Swirled and twirled around the church
  In Dippley Dockerlee!

Then Brother Davey Docker
  Who plays the organ, flew
Into the church at double-tick,
  Shouting, "I'll join in, too!"

He sat down at the organ
  And pumped without a doubt;
And as he played,
  "Let's Praise The Lord,"
    He blew Benjamin...
      SWOOSH!...RIGHT OUT!

So..........
  Praising God together
  Is what saved our little friend,
  And Benjamin would like to tell you
  To praise God from beginning to end!

    BUZZ-A-BUZZ-BUZZ...
    BUZZ-A-BUZZ-BUZZ...

That's Benjamin saying,
  "PRAISE THE LORD!
    GOODBYE!"

86

ONE, TWO

One, two, Jesus, I love you;
   Three, four, knock at my heart's door.
Five, six, I'll let you in quick;
   Seven, eight, You'll open Heaven's gate;
Nine, ten, I love you. Amen.

COCK-A-DOODLE-DO

Cock-a-doodle-do!
   If I just had a shoe
That lasted me for forty years,
   I'd cock-a-doodle, too!

SMILE AT YOUR ANGEL

Did you know
  That there are angels
Standing by you?
  Yes! It's so!
And although you cannot see them,
  They go everywhere you go.
They will watch you at the table,
  They will watch at night in bed;
They will watch when you are playing;
  They hear everything that's said.
So, when you wake up in the morning
  And look out at the sky,
Smile and say, "Good morning!"
  To your angel standing by.

WHEN DADDY PRAYS FOR ME

If I fall down and scrape my knee,
  I ask Daddy to pray for me.
It makes me feel so good and fine
  When his big hands fold over mine.
Or when he puts them on my head
  Before I jump into my bed.
I know that everything will be
  All right, when Daddy prays for me.

88

WEE WILLIE WINKIE

Wee Willie Winkie
  Runs through the town,
Upstairs and downstairs
  In his nightgown;
Rapping at the windows,
  Shouting through the locks,
"Have the children
  Said their prayers?
It's past eight o'clock!"

Wee Willie Winkie
  Runs through the town,
Asking moms and daddies
  In his nightgown,
"Did you tuck the children in
  And listen while they pray;
And ask the Lord to bless them
  Through the night and through the day?"

WOULD YOU PRAISE HIM ON A CACTUS?

Would you praise Him
On a cactus?
Would you praise Him
Just for practice?

Would you praise Him
In a hole?
Would you praise Him
On a pole?

DANDELION SEA

Would you praise Him
When you're small?
Would you praise Him
When you're tall?

Would you praise Him
In a tree?
Would you praise Him
On your knee?

Would you praise Him
On a roof?
Would you praise Him
With one tooth?

Would you praise Him
With a song?
Would you praise Him
With a gong?

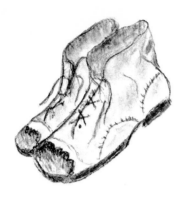

Would you praise Him
    In old shoes?
Would you praise Him
    When you lose?

Would you praise Him
    Beating drums?
Would you praise Him
    With smashed thumbs?

Would you praise Him
    On a sled?
Would you praise Him
    On your head?

Would you praise Him
   In a pew?
Would you praise Him
   In an igloo?

Would you praise Him
   With a clown?
Would you praise Him
   Round the town?

Would you praise Him
   When you're glad?
Would you praise Him
   When you're sad?

Would you praise Him
Blowing bubbles?
Would you praise Him
In your troubles?

Would you praise Him
With a dove?
Would you praise Him
For His love?

Would you praise Him
Hot or cooler?
YES! I'LL PRAISE HIM!
HALLELUJAH!

I HAD A LITTLE PONY

I had a little pony,
  His name was Dapple Gray.
I lent him to the Lord to ride
  Down into town, one day.
Jesus patted him and rode him,
  And people waved palm limbs.
Oh, I'd lend my pony any time
  That Jesus needed him!

SING A SONG OF SIXPENCE

Sing a song of sixpence,
  A pocket for the Lord;
Four and twenty children
  A penny could afford
To send across the ocean,
  For other children there
To learn about dear Jesus,
  Who answers every prayer.

JOSH'S 5,000 LUNCHES

Once upon a time
   There was a little boy named Josh.
He liked to go out fishing
   And splash and splush and splosh.

One day he took his pole,
   And his mother made a lunch,
Because young boys who fish and play
   Need something to munch and crunch.

Josh chased the little fishes
   Under rocks and down the stream,
But couldn't catch even one,
   As easy as that may seem!

He walked along the stream
  Making frizby-frozby noise,
But little fishes hide away
  From splashing, sploshing boys.

He sang, "Oh, Frizby and Frozby,
  I'll catch you if I can;
You cannot hide from me,
  For I'm a great fisherman."

97

He soon was tired and hungry,
   And said to those hiding fish,
"If you come up, I'll share my lunch,
   Five loaves and two little fish."

"Five loaves and two little fish
   You'll share?" a man said, suddenly;
"You're just the boy that Jesus needs.
   I'm Andrew—do come with me."

So little Josh jumped up
   And ran with Andrew on tip-toe,
Up to the hill where Jesus stood,
   With five thousand people below.

"Here's a boy, Lord Jesus,
   With a lunch of fish and bread.
Josh, would you give your lunch to Jesus
   To make five thousand lunches instead?"

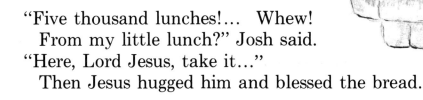

"Five thousand lunches!... Whew!
   From my little lunch?" Josh said.
"Here, Lord Jesus, take it..."
   Then Jesus hugged him and blessed the bread.

One...two...and a hundred,
   The lunch kept making more and more,
As Jesus passed it from His hands...
   Four thousand and forty-four!

At last 5,000 hungry people
  All ate their lunch that day,
From two little fish and five little loaves
  That Josh had given away.

Josh ran home so excited,
  He forgot to splash and splush.
The hiding fishes in the stream
  Said, "Josh is in such a rush!"

They heard him say, "Oh Frizby
  And oh, Frozby, you can hide;
I went fishing with Jesus today
  And my lunch was multiplied!"

Then he remembered his dear mommy
  Had packed the fish and bread,
So she had also helped the Lord
  And people who were fed.

"Oh, Mommy, Mommy!" he cried out,
  "When you made my lunch today,
You were really making 5,000 lunches
  For Jesus to give away!"

GRANDPA MOLE'S PARTY

"Hello children!

I'm knocking on the door of a strange little house.

It's down in the ground, under a big tree by the pond in Dandelion Sea.

It's Grandpa Mole's house!

He invited all of us to a party today. He loves to have parties for his dear friends. You are a dear friend of his and so am I!"

GRANDPA MOLE

Knock – knock – knock…ring-a-ling!…

"He must be very busy, so we'll ring again."

Ring-a-ling!…

"Boys and girls, will you help me call him?
I'm sure he'll hear if we both call out,
Grandpa Mole! We're here!"

"Thank you! Here he comes."

"Sorrabahum…Sorrabahum…"

(Remember, boys and girls, that's how
Grandpa Mole says, "Bless you, children.")

"Bless you, too, Grandpa Mole.
Thank you for inviting us to your party."

"What a cozy little house you have
All green and brown and red.
And a fireplace with an oven
Baking bingle-berry bread!"

Hmmmmm...fruits and nuts
And honey cones
For Benjamin Bumblebee.
And dandelion dandies
For Charlie Cricket, I see.

Well...here is Charlie now.
" Hello, Charlie...do come in!"
"Chirrup, chirrup, chirrup,
I've brought Lucy Ladybug's violin."

Here comes Lucy with Mrs. Mouse!
And Barney Beetle's bringing a cake.
Sammy and Mrs. Sparrow
Just flew in from Lily-pad Lake.

Luke and Larry Lightning Bug
Are lighting up the lamp.
And here is Benjamin Bumblebee
Buzzing in from Honeyrock Camp.

Hippity, Hoppity...Here's Brother Rabbit,
Now everyone is here.
"But what's that extra place for,
Grandpa Mole, and that special chair?"

"That place is set for Jesus,
We want Him to be our guest,
So we set a special place for Him,
Our very, very best!"

"Let's sing our prayer to thank Him
For bingle-berry bread."
"And dandelion dandies!"
Charlie Cricket said.

So we all sang together:

"Thank you, Lord, for bingle-berry bread,
  Bingle-berry bread,
  Bingle-berry bread.
Thank you, Lord, for bingle-berry bread,
  And for Grandpa Mole.
Come and be our special guest,
  Special guest, special guest.
Come and be our special guest,
  Lord Jesus, come, we pray."

103

And what a happy time everyone had!—
Singing, eating and playing games!

We all agreed that Grandpa Mole's house
Was one of the finest places in the whole world
To have a party.

Then Grandpa Mole said,
"I hope all of you wonderful girls and boys
Will have a special place for the Lord Jesus
At your next party."

"Sorrabahum.....Sorrabahum.....
Bless you, children."

"Bless you, too, dear Grandpa Mole,
And thank you for this lovely party!"

DID JESUS?

"Mommy," my Johnny asked one day,
  "When Jesus was a boy at play,
Did He chase a rabbit
  And catch a frog,
And did he have a little white dog?"

"Did He pick a daisy for His mommy dear?
  When he bumped His head,
Did He cry a tear?
  And when He was all tucked in bed,
  What were the stories
  His mommy read?
Did He sail a paper boat at sea,
  And do all those things...
  Just like me?"

"Did He help His daddy to cut some wood,
    And dig in the sand
As fast as He could?
    And when He looked up in the sky,
Did He wish to go up there and fly?
    Did He go out looking
    For a bird's nest?
Did He have to take a nap and rest?
    Did He love to climb up in a tree,
And do all those things…
    Just like me?"

"Yes, my Johnny,
    I'm sure it is true
That Jesus did all those things…
    Just like you."

RIDE A COCK-HORSE

Ride a cock-horse
　　To Banbury Cross,
To see all the children
　　Make music and sing.
With bells on their fingers
　　And bells on each toe,
They praise God with music
　　Wherever they go.

ONE, TWO, THREE, FOUR, FIVE

One, two, three, four, five,
　　Once I caught a fish alive;
Six, seven, eight, nine, ten,
　　Jesus said, "Now, fish for men!"
How can I catch men on a hook?
　　God tells you how in His Good Book.

OLD MOTHER GOOSE

Old Mother Goose,
  When she wanted to wander,
Would ride through the air
  On a very fine gander.

She'd fly to a house
  That stood in the wood,
To tell all the children
  That God is so good.

And then she would sing them
  A bright, happy tune,
That Jesus is coming
  Back to the earth soon!
And children who love Him
  Are never alone,
And will see him as King
  On a beautiful throne.

Then off on her gander
  She'd fly through the air
To far away places,
  To tell children there.

Old Mother Goose,
  One fine morning, I'm told,
Will find up in Heaven
  Her house made of gold!

CONTENTS

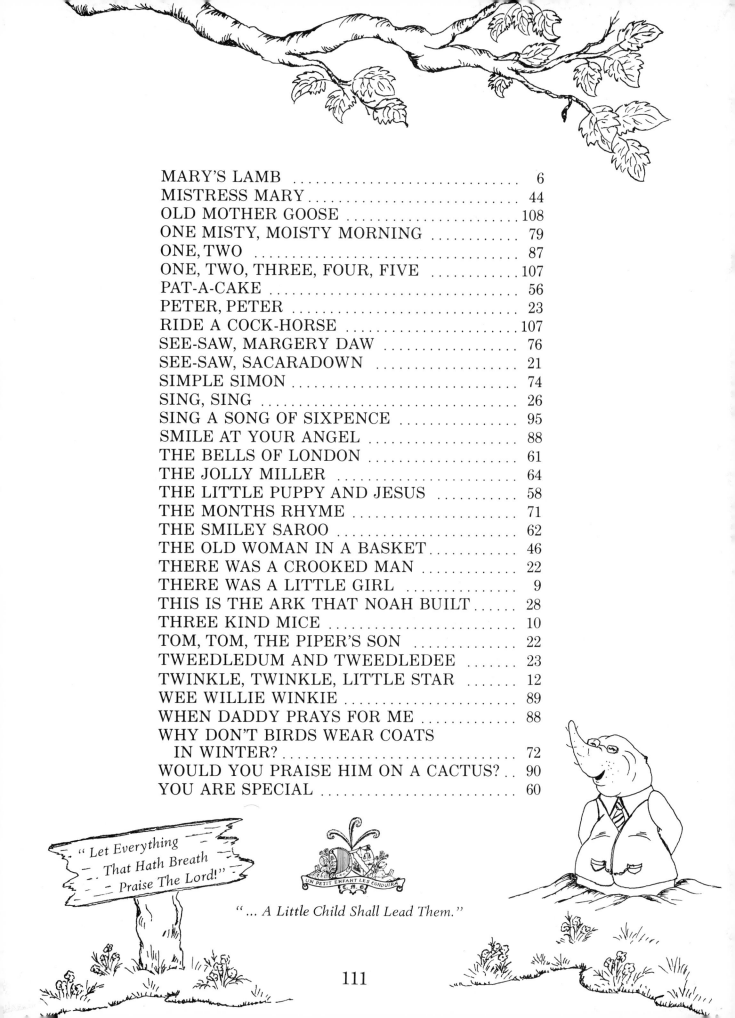

"Let Everything
That Hath Breath
Praise The Lord!"

"... A Little Child Shall Lead Them."

MARJORIE AINSBOROUGH DECKER

Marjorie Ainsborough Decker is originally from Liverpool, England, and has long been interested in the history of nursery rhyme.

Several years ago, she was given the title, "The Christian Mother Goose," by a little girl who had been listening to "TAPES FOR TOTS"—a "Christian Mother Goose" cassette series written and narrated by Marjorie. The title could not have been given to a more likely candidate.

Her love of writing "Once upon a time," began at eight years of age and in the ensuing years she has written poems, stories, songs and plays. She recently wrote and directed the full-scale Christian musical production, *A Day At Dandelion Sea*. Her husband Dale, is amused at the many water-smeared manuscripts she scribbles in the bath. And that is the spot where the idea first came for adapting traditional rhymes into a Christian setting; and where several of the stories in this book were written.

Marjorie also illustrated the traditional nursery rhymes in *The Christian Mother Goose Book*.

As an enthusiastic Christian and an ardent student of the Bible, she is a frequent guest speaker and singer at various conferences and churches. Dale and Marjorie Decker are the parents of four sons and live in Western Colorado.

Glenna Fae Hammond

Glenna Fae Hammond's accomplishment in the delightful illustrations of the Dandelion Sea characters in this book, is a story in itself.

She was paralyzed by a serious stroke after the birth of her last son. Although she miraculously recovered, she felt her artistic skill had been impaired. When she was called to consider developing dear, old Grandpa Mole, Charlie Cricket and other quaint people of Dandelion Sea, she quickly agreed to send some sketches. Her husband, Tom, came home to find her in tears as she faced the test of trying to draw again. With great confidence he encouraged her to pick up her pencil and begin.

The results of her fortitude and dedication delightfully parade through the pages of *The Christian Mother Goose Book*.

In the words of her husband, "Four years ago, my wife suffered a severe stroke and was totally paralyzed on her right side and unable to speak. Within six weeks she was home and caring for her family. We know that God has healed her and given to her a testimony of His goodness through this book."

Tom and Glenna Fae Hammond have three children and live in Eastern Colorado.